I DON'T LIKE BOOKS. NEVER. EVER. THE END.

Emma Perry & Sharon Davey

David Fickling Books

Once upon

a time

there was

a girl

called Mabel.

A girl who

didn't

like

books.

Never.

Ever.

THE END.

But . . .

the books just kept on coming.

She was given books on birthdays.
"A book? Oh, thanks?"

She was given
books as treats.
"Another book?"
Really?!"

She was even
given books . . .
just because.

"But I don't like books.

NEVER.

EVER.

The end!" declared Mabel.

Mabel used those books for many things.

She used them as a step to reach her Super Secret
Shelves. And as a doorstop to keep her brother out.

She even used them as a sledge to slide

bump bump bumpity bump

down the stairs.

But she couldn't be bothered
with the stories inside them.

Then one day, when she had . . .

slurped dinner
off two of them,

juggled with
three of them,

then made hats from
four of them . . .

Mabel's books decided that enough was enough.
They wanted to be read.

It was time for action!

So that night, as Mabel tried to get comfy
in her bed, something started to happen –

right

in the

corner

of her

room.

There was . . .

...a racket, a commotion,
a hullabaloo.

The noise grew,

and grew,

and grew,

until . . .

Books! Books! Everywhere!

They zoomed and zipped around the room.
They flipped
and flapped
above her head.

"GO AWAY!" shouted Mabel.
"I've got better things to do than bother with books!"

But the books flew faster, and the flapping
grew louder until Mabel started . . .

There was a rustling, a crackling,
a flick of a page and Mabel found herself . . .

. . . deep in the pages of an unread book.

"Yikes! Who are you?" asked Mabel.

"Hey, kid, watch it!" said a detective.

"I've a case to solve."

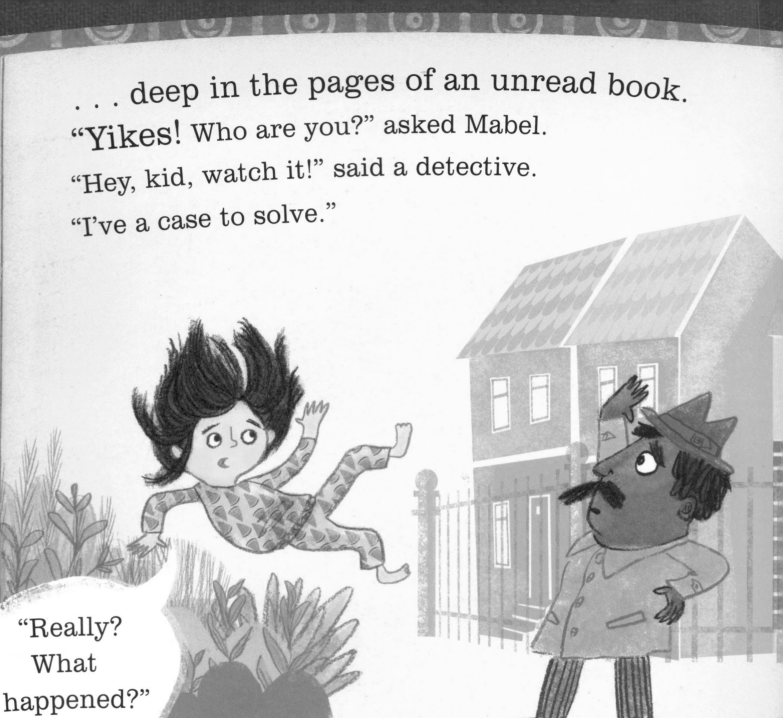

"Really? What happened?"

"Missing diamonds! You'll need to read the book to discover whodunnit . . ."

And the detective disappeared over the page.

"Wait!" cried Mabel.
"I'd be great at
solving crimes."

But Mabel was too late . . . There was a rustling, a crackling, a flick of a page and she found herself . . .

. . . in a spaceship.

"Mission control, we are ready for take-off,"
said the astronaut.

"A trip to the moon?"
said Mabel. "Let me come!
I love space . . ."

"This mission continues over the page,"
said the astronaut.
"5 . . . 4 . . . 3 . . . 2 . . ."

But Mabel was too late *again* . . .

There was a rustling,

a crackling,

a flick of a page

and she found herself . . . .

. . . on a drawbridge.

"Good day, young lady. Pray let us pass. We've castles to seek and dragons to duel," said the knight.

"Wow, really?! Can *I* come?"

"'Tis an unusual request from someone who didn't want to read our story!"

"This isn't fair!" said Mabel. "Exciting mysteries, space missions, and now your adventure – I **want** to join in."

"Indeed.'Tis a shame you've got better things to do than . . . *bother with books.*"

And the knight galloped off the edge of the page, leaving Mabel . . .

. . . alone.

On a blank page.

With no stories.
No adventures.

Nothing.

Just then, far in the distance,
Mabel could hear
a flapping.

It got
louder
and
louder

until she felt herself falling and falling . . .

. . . back into her bedroom.

She glanced
around, and
FINALLY

she saw **stories and adventures** piled all around her.

Mabel picked up a book, then snuggled under the covers. She discovered the stories tucked inside.

The words. The adventures.
EVERYTHING!

Once upon

a time

there was

a girl

called Mabel.

A girl

who loved

books.

Forever

and

ever.

THE END.

*Hi Kieran! *waves* * Hi Mabel! *waves* E.P.*

To Neve and Alex, always. S.D.

I DON'T LIKE BOOKS. NEVER. EVER. THE END.
is a DAVID FICKLING BOOK
First published in Great Britain in 2020 by
David Fickling Books,
31 Beaumont Street,
Oxford, OX1 2NP

978 1 788450 61 4

www.davidficklingbooks.com

Text © Emma Perry, 2020
Illustrations © Sharon Davey, 2020

3 5 7 9 10 8 6 4 2

The right of Emma Perry to be identified as the author and Sharon Davey
to be identified as the illustrator of this work has been asserted
in accordance with the Copyright, Designs and Patents Act 1988.

WARNING: This book will whisk you off on amazing adventures . . .

Papers used by David Fickling Books are from well-managed forests
and other responsible sources.

MIX
Paper from
responsible sources
FSC® C126477
FSC
www.fsc.org

DAVID FICKLING BOOKS Reg. No. 8340307

A CIP catalogue record for this book is available
from the British Library.

Printed in Slovenia by Abografika

Edited by Alice Corrie & designed by Ness Wood